Santa Claus Is Comin' to Town

By J. Fred Coots and Haven Gillespie.

Copyright © 1934, renewed 1962 by Leo Feist Inc. and Haven Gillespie
Music. All rights for the United States controlled and administered by EMI
Feist Catalog Inc. and Haven Gillespie Music. Rights assigned to EMI Catalogue
Partnership. All rights for the world excluding United States controlled and
administered by EMI Feist Catalog Inc. All rights reserved / International copyright
secured / Used by permission.

Illustrations copyright © 2004 by Steven Kellogg

Manufactured in China by South China Printing Company Ltd. All rights reserved.

www.harperchildrens.com

Library of Congress Cataloging-in-Publication Data

Kellogg, Steven.

Santa Claus is comin' to town / written by J. Fred Coots & Haven Gillespie ;
illustrated by Steven Kellogg.—1st ed.   p.   cm.

ISBN 0-688-14938-3 — ISBN 0-06-623849-8 (lib. bdg.)

1. Children's songs—United States—Texts. [1. Santa Claus—Songs and music.
2. Christmas music. 3. Songs.] I. Gillespie, Haven, 1888–1975 Santa Claus is
comin' to town. II. Title.

PZ8.3.K33San 2004

782.42'1723—dc21   2003001821

Typography by Martha Rago and Amelia Anderson

1 2 3 4 5 6 7 8 9 10 ❖ First Edition

To Helen, with love

Santa Claus Is Comin' to Town

Written by
J. Fred Coots & Haven Gillespie

illustrated by Steven Kellogg

HarperCollinsPublishers

I just came back
from a lovely trip
Along the Milky Way,
I stopped off at the
North Pole
To spend a holiday;

I called on
dear old
Santa Claus
To see what
I could see,

He took me to
his workshop

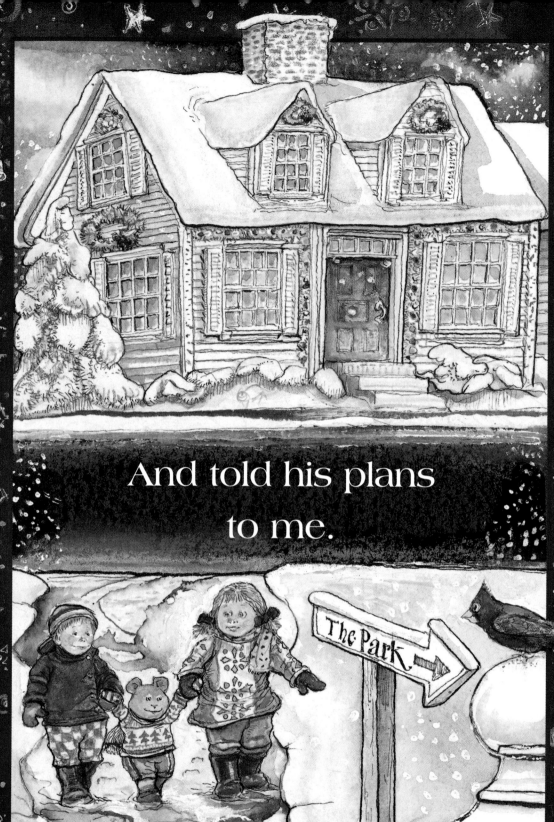

And told his plans
to me.

OH! You better watch out,
you better not cry,

Better not pout,
I'm telling you why:

Santa Claus is comin' to town.

He's making a list and checking it twice,

Gonna find out who's naughty and nice,

Santa Claus is comin' to town.

NORTH POLE

He sees you when you're sleepin',

He knows when you're awake,

He knows if you've been bad

No!

or good,

Please may I help?

So be good for goodness sake.

OH! You better watch out, you better not cry,
Better not pout, I'm telling you why:

Santa Claus is comin' to town.

With little tin horns and little toy drums,

Rooty-toot-toots and rummy-tum-tums,

Santa Claus is comin'

TO TOWN

And curly head dolls that toddle and coo,

Elephants,

kiddie cars too,

Santa Claus is comin' to **TOWN**

PLEASE
SLOW DOWN

The Kids in Girl- and Boyland will have a jubilee,

They're gonna build a Toyland town

all around the Christmas tree.

Because he's getting ready

Now Santa is a busy man,
He has no time to play

You'd better write your letter now

So,

His reindeers and his sleigh.

You better watch out,
you better not cry,
Better not pout,
I'm telling you why:

Santa Claus is comin' to town.